High Scorer

"What's your score?" Todd asked.

Yawning, Elizabeth pressed the Hall of Fame button on her video game. "Twenty-two thousand, five hundred points," she said proudly. "I played under the covers last night with a flashlight after I went to bed."

"Pretty good," Todd said.

"Pretty good," Andy agreed. "But I'm up to twenty-three thousand points. That means I'm ahead of both of you."

"Really?" Elizabeth covered her mouth with one hand while she yawned again. She couldn't believe Andy was still beating her best scores. "Well, I'm getting better, so watch out!"

Bantam Skylark Books in the
SWEET VALLEY KIDS series

SWEET VALLEY KIDS

ELIZABETH'S VIDEO FEVER

Written by
Molly Mia Stewart

Created by
FRANCINE PASCAL

Illustrated by
Ying-Hwa Hu

A BANTAM SKYLARK BOOK ®
NEW YORK • TORONTO • LONDON • SYDNEY • AUCKLAND

RL 2, 005–008

ELIZABETH'S VIDEO FEVER

A Bantam Skylark Book / February 1993

*Sweet Valley High® and Sweet Valley Kids are trademarks of
Francine Pascal*

Conceived by Francine Pascal

*Produced by Daniel Weiss Associates, Inc.
33 West 17th Street
New York, NY 10011*

Cover art by Susan Tang

*Skylark Books is a registered trademark of Bantam Books, a division
of Bantam Doubleday Dell Publishing Group, Inc.
Registered in U.S. Patent and Trademark Office
and elsewhere.*

ISBN 0-553-48010-3

Published simultaneously in the United States and Canada

Bantam Books are published by Bantam Books, a division of Bantam
Dell Publishing Group, Inc. Its trademark, consisting of the words
"Bantam Books" and the portrayal of a rooster, is Registered in U.S.
Patent and Trademark Office and in other countries. Marca Registrada.
Bantam Books, 666 Fifth Avenue, New York, NY 10103.

PRINTED IN THE UNITED STATES OF AMERICA

CWO   0   9   8   7   6   5   4   3   2   1

To Skylor Cameron Waller

CHAPTER 1

Goin' Wild

Elizabeth Wakefield walked slowly toward the bus stop. She was hardly even looking where she was going because she was so busy staring down at the bleeping video game in her hands. "I got one!" she yelled.

"Big deal," said her twin sister, Jessica. "Why do you play that silly 'Goin' Wild' game all the time?"

"Because it's fun, that's why," Elizabeth said, not taking her eyes off her new hand-held video game for a second. "It's really, really fun."

Jessica made a face. "You could have fooled me."

Jessica and Elizabeth didn't always agree on everything, even though they were identical twins. Some people thought that the twins were exactly alike, because they looked alike on the outside. They both had long blond hair and blue-green eyes. When they wore identical outfits to school, even their closest friends had trouble telling them apart.

But the twins were very different on the inside. Elizabeth loved sports, especially soccer. She also liked to climb trees and play in the fort she had built in the backyard. Jessica liked the fort, too, but she usually preferred to play inside so that she wouldn't get her clothes messy. She enjoyed playing with her stuffed animals and rearranging the furniture in the twins' dollhouse.

But even though they couldn't always agree on what to play, the twins always agreed that they were best friends. And usually they could figure out a game that they both liked so that they could play together.

But that was before Elizabeth got "Goin' Wild." She had saved up her Christmas money to buy it, and now she played it all the time. To win the game you had to get a little camper to his tent. On the way, the camper had to cross rivers, run from bears, and zap mosquitoes. Jessica had tried it a few times, but she thought it was boring. Elizabeth loved it, though. She had already reached the second level of difficulty. More than anything, she wanted to get to level five, the highest level.

"You only got that video game because Todd and Andy both have one," Jessica said with a pout. "Why do you want to be as good as them, anyway?"

Elizabeth shrugged. Then her camper fell into the river, and the game was over. "Because it's fun," she said again with a smile as they reached the bus stop.

"Hey, Elizabeth," Todd Wilkins shouted. He was in the twins' class, and he and Elizabeth were good friends.

"What's your high score? I'm up to twelve thousand, five hundred points."

"Really? I'm only up to ten thousand," Elizabeth said. "But—"

"Here comes the bus," Jessica interrupted.

"Sit with me," Todd said to Elizabeth. "I'll show you a trick for getting away from the grizzly bears in level two."

Elizabeth looked at Jessica. The twins almost always sat together on the bus. But Elizabeth wanted to see how good Todd was getting at "Goin' Wild." She knew her sister would understand.

Elizabeth and Todd played their video games all the way to school. Elizabeth was still concentrating on getting to level three as she walked into her classroom.

She pressed a button just as the camper reached a stream. Instead of falling into the water, the camper hopped from one stepping-stone to the next, until he reached the other side.

"Yes!" Elizabeth cheered, holding up her game. "I got one hundred bonus points."

Mrs. Otis looked up from her desk. "What's so exciting, Elizabeth?"

Elizabeth put the game behind her back and smiled guiltily at her teacher. "Nothing, Mrs. Otis."

"Don't get too caught up in that game, now," Mrs. Otis said. "You don't want to stop reading books or playing with your friends."

"Don't worry, Mrs. Otis," Elizabeth said. "I won't."

She hurried to her seat and quickly entered her initials in her game's "Hall of Fame." Then she turned around to show Todd.

"I'm going to get the highest score," she told him with a smile. "Wait and see."

CHAPTER 2

The Contest

After Mrs. Otis took attendance, she made an announcement.

"There's going to be a writing contest," she said. "The theme is Valentine's Day. You can write a story, a poem, or an essay to enter. Winners will be chosen in each grade."

"Psst," Jessica whispered, leaning over to her sister, "Are you going to enter the contest?"

"Sure," Elizabeth whispered back. "It's easy to write about Valentine's Day."

Jessica slumped down in her chair. She loved contests, but she knew that Elizabeth was the best writer in their class. Jessica was sure that she could never write a better story or poem than Elizabeth, so she decided she wouldn't even try.

At recess, she got on the swings with her friends Lila Fowler and Ellen Riteman. "What are you going to write about for the contest?" Lila asked.

Jessica shrugged. "Nothing. I can never win if Elizabeth enters."

"I bet Elizabeth will write a love story about her video game," Ellen said.

"Ha ha, very funny," Jessica said.

"She sure does play with it a lot," Lila said. "It's kind of weird."

They all looked over to the jungle gym, where Elizabeth, Todd, and Andy were sitting. They were all busy playing with their "Goin' Wild" games.

"Is she turning into some kind of nerd?" Ellen asked with a giggle.

Jessica felt her cheeks get hot. "Elizabeth is not weird and she's not a nerd," she said loudly. She jumped off her swing and walked across the playground to the jungle gym. Elizabeth, Todd, and Andy were all staring seriously at their games without speaking. The only noise was the bleeping of the sound effects. Elizabeth's thumbs jabbed at the game buttons, and Andy kept nodding his head each time he

zapped something. None of them even noticed that Jessica was there.

"Liz, do you want to go on the swings?" Jessica asked.

"Maybe later," Elizabeth said, not looking up. "I'm right in the middle of a game."

"Got it," Andy shouted suddenly. He looked up at the others and grinned, pushing his glasses up on his nose. "Only three hundred more points and I'll be on level three."

Elizabeth smiled at Andy. "Don't worry. I'll catch up with you soon."

"Me, too," Todd added. "I'm going to be the first one to reach level five."

Andy grinned. "Don't bet on it. I'm almost there."

Jessica glared at Andy. He had been the first one to get the game. So Jessica blamed him for the way Elizabeth was acting.

"How about going on the seesaw?" she asked Elizabeth.

"In a little while," Elizabeth answered. "I want to see if I can beat my high score. Oh, no! There's a whole bunch of mosquitoes coming after me."

Jessica shoved her hands in her pockets and put on a sad, lonely expression. If she really tried hard, she could even make a few tears come to her eyes. But Elizabeth wasn't even looking at her. Feeling very grumpy, Jessica turned and stomped away.

14

CHAPTER 3

Elizabeth's Promise

When Elizabeth got home after school, she went straight upstairs. She sat down at her desk and took out a notebook.

"Are you starting your homework now?" Jessica asked. "I'm going outside."

"Go ahead. I want to get started on my story for the Valentine's Day writing contest," Elizabeth answered. She opened her notebook to a clean page as Jessica left the room.

Usually, it was easy for Elizabeth to think of things to write about. But at the moment, she didn't have any ideas. All she could think about was the little camper from "Goin' Wild." She had almost reached Andy's highest score. All she had to do was climb the muddy mountain, fill the canteen with water from the stream, and get back to the tent. Then she could go on to level three.

Elizabeth put down her pencil, opened her backpack, and took out her video game. As soon as she turned it on, she forgot all about the writing contest.

"Elizabeth! Elizabeth!" Mrs. Wakefield called much later.

Startled, Elizabeth put down the game and ran to the door. "What, Mom?"

"It's time for dinner," her mother said from downstairs. "Isn't it your turn to set the table?"

Elizabeth felt her stomach do a flip-flop. She never forgot to do her chores. "Sorry, Mom," she said, hurrying down the stairs. "I was—busy doing something."

Mrs. Wakefield stood in the hallway. "I'm very surprised at you, Elizabeth. I've been calling you for five minutes. When you didn't answer I thought you must have fallen asleep."

Elizabeth felt even worse. "I'm sorry," she repeated. She quickly set the table, and then took her seat without speaking.

"What's new in school?" Mr. Wakefield asked when everyone had sat down.

Steven, the twins' older brother, took a large gulp of milk from his glass. "There's a writing contest," he said. "For *Valentine's* Day. Gross."

"I think that's a nice theme for a writing contest, Steven," Mrs. Wakefield said, laughing. "And a pretty easy one, too."

Mr. Wakefield smiled at Elizabeth. "Our expert writer here could probably write a great story on any subject at all with no trouble. I'll bet we can't name a subject too hard for Elizabeth to write about."

"Cement," Jessica suggested. "I bet even Liz couldn't write something good about cement. Or mud."

"Mud would be easy," Elizabeth said with a giggle. "I could write a story about making mud pies."

"See?" Mr. Wakefield said proudly. "Elizabeth can write about anything."

"I'm sure you'll come up with a terrific idea for the contest, won't you?" Mrs. Wakefield said.

Elizabeth nodded. "I'll try."

"How about you, Jessica?" Mr. Wakefield asked. "You've got a pretty active imagination, too. Are you going to write something?"

Jessica looked down at her plate. "I don't think so."

"I'll help you, if you want," Elizabeth offered.

"That's very nice of you, Elizabeth," Mrs. Wakefield said.

Elizabeth smiled. "No problem. That way, we can both enter the contest. OK, Jess?"

Jessica looked uncertain. "OK. That'd be great. But are you sure you want to help me?"

"Absolutely." Elizabeth crossed her heart and snapped her fingers twice. That was the twins' special promise sign. And Elizabeth had never broken a promise yet.

CHAPTER 4

Forgotten Friends

Jessica looked over at Elizabeth as the final bell rang at the end of school the next day. "Let's hurry so we get a good seat on the bus," she said.

Elizabeth took "Goin' Wild" out of her desk and put it in her backpack. "Amy's coming over to play today," she reminded Jessica. "We can sit three in a seat."

Amy Sutton was one of Elizabeth's best friends. Jessica liked her, too. She was especially glad that Amy was coming over today, because it meant that Elizabeth wouldn't be able to play her video game all afternoon.

"Come on," Elizabeth called out to Amy.

The three girls ran down the hall and scrambled into the bus waiting for them outside. They all squeezed into a seat together.

"What should we do when we get home?" Jessica asked.

"Let's play in the fort. We can pretend we're pirates," Amy suggested.

"OK," Elizabeth agreed. "But don't you want to try my video game, Amy? It's really fun."

"Oh, brother," Jessica said under her breath.

Amy shrugged. "Sure, I guess so. I don't know if I'm any good, but I'll try."

Elizabeth held the game out to her friend, but then took it back immediately. "Let me just show you what to do," she said, switching on the power. "There's this really excellent part in level two."

Jessica sighed and looked out the window for the whole bus ride. Instead of letting Amy have a turn with "Goin' Wild," Elizabeth just kept showing Amy how to play. The one time Jessica glanced over at Amy, she noticed that Amy looked bored.

"It's just like any other video game," Amy said once they were off the bus and walking toward the Wakefield house.

Elizabeth was moving her feet slowly, playing the game as she walked. "No, it's

not. It's more fun. Oops! I fell into the river again."

Amy looked at Jessica, and Jessica looked back at Amy. Jessica had a feeling she was going to be playing with Amy by herself all afternoon.

"Come on, Amy," Jessica said in a grumpy voice. "We'll have a snack and then play with the dollhouse."

"What did you say?" Elizabeth asked from behind them. She was staring hard at the game.

"Nothing," Amy answered for Jessica. "You wouldn't care, anyway." Elizabeth was too absorbed to hear Amy, so she didn't answer.

Jessica shrugged as she opened the

front door. "Stupid old game," she muttered.

"Why does Elizabeth like it so much?" Amy asked.

"I guess she likes zapping mosquitoes," Jessica said, heading toward the kitchen. "And she wants to beat Todd and Andy."

"Big deal," Amy said.

"Yeah, big deal." Jessica let out a sigh. "Who cares?"

By the time Amy went home, Jessica was in a very bad mood. Elizabeth was still sitting in the living room, punching away at the buttons on her video game. Jessica walked into the den to watch television.

But as she sat down on the couch, she

noticed that the wastebasket by the fireplace was full. It was one of Elizabeth's chores for the month to empty the wastebaskets. Jessica wondered if Elizabeth would get in trouble for not doing it. She hoped not. Their mother had already scolded Elizabeth for not setting the table.

"Liz?" Jessica called.

"Wait a second, I'll be right there," Elizabeth answered from the living room.

Jessica waited, but after several minutes had gone by, she gave up. She quickly grabbed the wastebaskets from the den and the kitchen and went out to the garage to empty them. Mr. Wakefield drove up just as she put the lid back on the garbage can.

"Hello, Elizabeth," Mr. Wakefield said. "Have a good day at school?"

"Daddy!" Jessica replied with a frown.

"Oh, sorry, Jessica," her father said. He looked puzzled. "Why are *you* emptying the wastebaskets? Isn't that Elizabeth's job?"

Jessica crossed her fingers behind her back. "I just wanted to help."

"Good girl," Mr. Wakefield said, giving her a kiss.

As he went inside, Jessica looked at the garbage can. More than anything else, she wished she could throw "Goin' Wild" inside and slam down the lid.

CHAPTER 5

A Bad Grade

Elizabeth walked into the classroom the next morning and sat down at her desk. Andy and Todd walked over to talk to her.

"What's your high score?" Todd asked.

Yawning, Elizabeth pressed the Hall of Fame button. "Twenty-two thousand, five hundred points," she said proudly. "I played under the covers last night with a flashlight after I went to bed."

"Pretty good," Todd said.

"Pretty good," Andy agreed. He smiled. "But I'm up to twenty-three thousand points. That means I'm ahead of both of you."

"Really?" Elizabeth covered her mouth with one hand while she yawned again. She couldn't believe Andy was still beating her best scores. "Well, I'm getting better, so watch out."

"Ahem! Please sit down everyone," said Mrs. Otis, walking to the front of the room. "It's time to get to work. I have spelling tests to hand back."

"Can I hand them out?" Caroline Pearce called from her seat. She was always trying to be the teacher's pet. She also liked to be able to see what grades everyone got.

Mrs. Otis handed her the papers. "Thank you for volunteering. Almost everyone in the class did very well."

Elizabeth smiled. She expected to get her usual grade of ninety-five or one-hundred percent. But when she got her test back, she couldn't believe her eyes. Her grade was an eighty! She looked over at Jessica. "What did you get?" she asked her sister.

"Eighty-five," Jessica said.

Feeling embarrassed, Elizabeth covered her grade with her hand. She hadn't gotten below a ninety in a long time, and she almost always got better grades than Jessica did, because Jessica didn't like to

31

study. Elizabeth knew that she had to do better next time, just the way she had to do better when she played her video game. Otherwise, she'd never get to level five.

"Elizabeth?" Mrs. Otis asked later that morning. "I asked you a question."

Elizabeth looked up in surprise. She was so sleepy that she wasn't sure what word they were on in the vocabulary list. "I'm sorry. What was the question?"

"I said, please define the word 'quantity'," Mrs. Otis repeated.

"It's, um . . ." Elizabeth searched her memory, but she couldn't remember the word.

"Anyone else?" the teacher asked after a pause.

Jessica raised her hand. "It means the amount of something," she said.

"That's correct," Mrs. Otis said. "Very good." She looked at Elizabeth. "Are you feeling sick, Elizabeth?"

Elizabeth shook her head quickly. "No, Mrs. Otis. I'm OK."

She opened her vocabulary book and promised herself that she would pay very careful attention for the rest of class. She kept looking at the clock, though, waiting for recess. As soon as she got out to the playground, she would try her hardest to beat Andy's score.

But when the bell rang and everyone stood up to go outside, Mrs. Otis called Elizabeth up to her desk.

"Elizabeth," the teacher said. "I want to talk to you about your schoolwork."

"My schoolwork?" Elizabeth repeated.

Mrs. Otis nodded. "For the last few days, your work has been quite a bit below your usual level. I'm very surprised at the homework papers you have turned in."

Elizabeth could feel her face turning red. She had never been scolded about her schoolwork in her whole life. She couldn't think of anything to say.

"Is something at home worrying you?" Mrs. Otis asked.

"No," Elizabeth said quietly.

"And you don't feel sick?" her teacher went on.

Elizabeth shook her head. "No."

"Well, I'm going to have to call your mother this afternoon and discuss this with her," Mrs. Otis said.

"No!" Elizabeth cried. "Please don't call my mother, Mrs. Otis. I'll do better. I promise."

Mrs. Otis shook her head. "I'm sorry, Elizabeth. But I'm very concerned about your work, and I think your parents should know."

Elizabeth was afraid she might begin to cry. She felt frightened and ashamed. She *never* got into trouble. But now Mrs. Otis was going to call her mother. It was a terrible feeling.

"Can I go out to the playground now?" Elizabeth asked quietly.

"I'd like you to stay in for recess today,"

Mrs. Otis said. "You can get a head start on your homework."

Elizabeth turned around and walked slowly back to her desk. Now she wouldn't be able to play "Goin' Wild" until after school.

CHAPTER 6

All Alone

Jessica had been standing outside the classroom door while Mrs. Otis scolded Elizabeth. She felt sorry for her sister. But she was angry, too. She ran out to the playground and saw Andy and Todd playing their video games.

"You two are so dumb," she yelled at them.

Todd and Andy looked up at her in surprise. "What's wrong?" Todd said. "We didn't do anything to you."

"You got my sister in trouble, that's what's wrong," Jessica said.

Andy blinked his eyes behind his glasses. "How?"

"You and your stupid game," Jessica said. "I hate 'Goin' Wild'!"

She turned and ran away. She didn't want the boys to see that she was beginning to cry. Sniffling hard, Jessica sat down against a brick wall and put her head down on her arms.

"Hi, Jessica," said a friendly voice.

Jessica looked up and saw Eva Simpson standing in front of her. "Hi, Eva," she mumbled.

Eva sat down next to her. "You look sad. Is something wrong?"

Jessica sniffed again. "I miss Elizabeth," she said. "Ever since she bought that silly video game, that's all she ever thinks about. She doesn't play with me anymore."

"Not at all?" Eva asked, her eyes widening.

"No." Jessica shook her head. "She keeps saying she will, but then she starts playing 'Goin' Wild' and she forgets all about me."

"That's not nice," Eva said. "You know what you could do?"

Jessica looked at Eva hopefully. "Hide her game?"

"No. You could write about missing

Elizabeth for the writing contest," Eva suggested.

"But the writing contest is supposed to be about Valentine's Day," Jessica reminded her.

Eva nodded. "Valentine's Day is about people you love. You love Elizabeth. My mother always says it's good to talk about the things that make you sad. Then sometimes you can figure out how to make them better."

"Really?" Jessica wasn't sure Eva's idea would work.

But then she looked over and saw Andy and Todd again. So far, nothing had been able to make Elizabeth stop playing her video game. Jessica was willing to try almost anything that might change that.

CHAPTER 7

Caught!

Elizabeth walked home from the bus stop as slowly as she could that afternoon. This time it wasn't because she was playing with her video game. She was just scared to face her mother.

"Hurry up," Jessica said, looking back at her. "It won't be that bad."

"I'm coming." Elizabeth gulped as she looked at their house. Then the front door opened, and Mrs. Wakefield came out to meet them.

"Elizabeth, we need to have a talk," she said in a no-nonsense voice.

Elizabeth and Jessica shared a worried look, and then Elizabeth followed Mrs. Wakefield inside and into the den. She sat down on the edge of the couch.

"Mrs. Otis called today," Mrs. Wakefield said. "I think you know what she wanted to talk about."

"Yes," Elizabeth whispered.

"She tells me you've been playing with your video game every spare moment. She's afraid you're doing it at home, too," Mrs. Wakefield said sternly. "Have you been playing 'Goin' Wild' when you should have been working on your homework?"

Elizabeth looked down at her feet. "Well, um . . ."

"Elizabeth, I'm very disappointed," Mrs. Wakefield said. "Have you even begun writing a story for Valentine's Day yet?"

Elizabeth felt so ashamed that she wanted to cry. She couldn't admit to her mother that she hadn't written a single word. That would only disappoint her even more.

Elizabeth put one hand behind her back and crossed her fingers. "Yes," she said, not looking at her mother.

It wasn't exactly a lie, she told herself. She was sure she would be able to write something good very easily. She always could.

Mrs. Wakefield stood up and went to the door. "Elizabeth, I think you should put away your game for a while."

"But, Mom—" Elizabeth began.

"I don't want you to play it for a week," Mrs. Wakefield said. "Your homework comes first."

"OK," Elizabeth whispered.

"Now go on upstairs and get started on your homework," Mrs. Wakefield said as she left the den.

Elizabeth walked slowly out of the den and up the stairs. "Did you get in trouble?" Jessica asked when Elizabeth entered their room.

"Yes," Elizabeth said, trying not to cry.

She put her backpack down on her desk. "I'm not allowed to play my video game for a week. And I have to do my homework right now. I can't play."

Jessica nodded. "I'm sorry," she said. "A week isn't so bad, though."

"That's easy for you to say," Elizabeth said.

Jessica didn't answer. She just shrugged and headed outside to play.

When Elizabeth was alone, she tried as hard as she could to make up a story for the writing contest. She opened her notebook to a fresh page and wrote her name at the top in her best handwriting. But she couldn't think of any ideas.

Finally, she took her pencil sharpener out of the drawer and sharpened her pencil. She wrote "Valentine's Day Story" under her name.

But she still couldn't think of a story.

Instead, she kept thinking about "Goin' Wild." She had almost reached level four that morning. She was sure that she could get there the next time she played. But if she had to wait an entire week, she would be completely out of practice. There was even the chance that she might not be able to pick up at the same level. She just had to play it one more time—then she would put it away.

Elizabeth glanced over her shoulder. There wasn't a sound anywhere in the house. Very quietly, she opened her backpack and took out the video game.

Then she turned down the volume on the game so that it would be silent.

She switched the power on.

At first, Elizabeth was too nervous about getting caught to do well. She kept making silly mistakes. With a frown, she concentrated harder on the game. Soon, she had forgotten everything else.

Elizabeth leaned forward eagerly, jabbing the buttons with her thumbs. Her score kept climbing higher and higher, until she finally reached level four.

"Yes!" she exclaimed, bouncing up and down on her chair.

She kept playing. Reaching level five seemed easy now. But she soon used up all her chances. Still, her score was the highest ever. It was higher than any score Andy or Todd had ever reached.

"Wait until they see this," Elizabeth whispered happily. She entered her initials in the "Hall of Fame." She couldn't wait to show the boys her score: fifty thousand points!

She held up the video game so she could look at the "Hall of Fame" herself.

And then Jessica and Mrs. Wakefield walked into the room.

CHAPTER 8

Jessica's Story

Jessica's eyes opened wide with shock when she saw Elizabeth holding "Goin' Wild." Then she looked quickly at Mrs. Wakefield.

Mrs. Wakefield did not look pleased.

"Elizabeth," she said firmly. "What did I tell you?"

Elizabeth swallowed but didn't say a word. Jessica could tell that her sister was about to burst into tears.

"Please give me the video game, Elizabeth," Mrs. Wakefield said, holding out her hand.

Without a word, Elizabeth stood up and handed the game to her mother. Then she stared glumly at the floor.

"Your father and I are going to have to talk about this when he gets home," Mrs. Wakefield went on. "We'll decide what to do then. Right now I hope you realize that it was wrong to disobey me."

"I'm sorry, Mom," Elizabeth choked out. "I didn't mean to."

"Have you done your homework yet?" Mrs. Wakefield asked. "Have you started your story?"

Sniffling, Elizabeth shook her head.

Jessica couldn't believe her ears. Usually, *she* was the one who got into trouble. Elizabeth was always obedient and cooperative. But now Elizabeth was actually in trouble for disobeying and not doing her homework. It felt very strange.

"All I can say is that I'm very upset," Mrs. Wakefield said. She left the room, pulling the door closed behind her.

Jessica watched in silence as Elizabeth went to her desk and sat down. She didn't know what to say.

The reason she had come upstairs was to ask Elizabeth for help. She had begun a story for the writing contest, but she was afraid that now Elizabeth was probably too upset to want to help.

Jessica looked down at her story. She had written about how much time identical twins usually spent together, and how lonely she felt since Elizabeth had started playing "Goin' Wild." It ended with the wish that Elizabeth would realize that a twin sister was more important than a video game, and stop ignoring Jessica.

Jessica didn't know if her story was any good. And she wasn't sure she wanted Elizabeth to read it. After all, the story was *about* Elizabeth. Jessica put it down on her desk and glanced over at her sister. Elizabeth still hadn't said anything.

Finally, the silence began to bother Jessica. "Why did you play 'Goin' Wild' when you weren't supposed to?" she asked.

"I don't know," Elizabeth said softly. "It was really stupid."

"Did you write anything at all yet?"

Jessica asked. She still couldn't believe that she had finished an assignment before Elizabeth had even begun.

"No, and I can't think of anything," Elizabeth cried. She stood up and started to walk around the room, as though that would give her an idea.

"Did you write anything?" Elizabeth asked, stopping in front of Jessica.

Jessica looked down at her paper. "Well . . ." The more she thought about it, the more she didn't want Elizabeth to read her story.

But before she realized it, Elizabeth had picked it up.

CHAPTER 9

Elizabeth's Story

Elizabeth read Jessica's story with a sinking feeling in her stomach. She felt terrible when she suddenly realized that her video game had indeed become more important to her than her sister, and that she had broken her promise to help Jessica with her writing.

"I'm sorry," she said, looking at Jessica. "I didn't know I was hurting your feelings."

Jessica still looked worried. "That's OK," she said. "But are you going to keep playing that game? I mean, when Mom finally gives it back to you?"

"No," Elizabeth said, shaking her head. "Now I don't even know why I liked it so much. Who cares who gets the highest score, anyway?"

"Do you mean it?" Jessica said in surprise. "You don't care about doing better than Todd and Andy?"

Elizabeth shook her head. "No. I must have been crazy! I'm in all this trouble because of that game, but I didn't see how dumb it was until I read your story."

Jessica let out a sigh of relief. "Good."

Smiling, Elizabeth sat down at her desk. "I just had a great idea for a story."

Without wasting another moment, she picked up her pencil and began to write.

Her story was called "Goin' Wild." The main character was the camper of the game, a girl she named Emily. There was one major difference from the game, however. Emily's parents and sister were with her. They were all supposed to work together to reach the campsite. But Emily ran ahead. She wanted to cross the rivers, zap the mosquitoes, and do everything alone. The more her family called for her to come back, the faster Emily ran. Soon she became lost in the woods.

For days and days, Emily wandered alone in the woods. She fell into rivers and was bitten by mosquitoes. Then there was a terrifying roar. A grizzly bear was

after her! Screaming, Emily ran as fast as she could. But the grizzly bear was catching up.

Then, up ahead, she heard voices.

"We're here, Emily. Hurry!" called her parents.

They were all up in a tree, safe from the grizzly bear. "Climb up!" her sister yelled. "You can do it."

Emily ran to the tree, but she couldn't reach the branches. "Please help," she shouted.

Her parents reached down to her. Emily grabbed their hands, and they pulled her up to safety just in time.

"I'm sorry for what I did," Emily told her family. "I never knew how much I loved you all until I got lost. Now I'll never go wild again!"

Together, the whole family made it to the campsite, and they had a Valentine's Day cookout.

When she finished, Elizabeth took a deep breath and put down her pencil. Then she carefully read her story again to check for mistakes, and copied it over in her best handwriting.

Even if she didn't hand it in for the writing contest, she was glad she had written it. Maybe it would tell her family just how she felt.

CHAPTER 10

Cured

"I want to read something," Elizabeth told the family at dinner that night. "It's my story for the writing contest. "I want you all to hear it. It's very important."

Mr. Wakefield looked surprised. "OK. If you think it's important, Elizabeth, go ahead."

Jessica took a swallow of milk, and

then listened while Elizabeth read. At first, she felt a little bit confused and angry that Elizabeth was *still* thinking about "Goin' Wild." But then she realized that the character of Emily was really Elizabeth, and that Elizabeth was describing herself in the story. The dining room was completely silent except for Elizabeth's voice.

At last, Elizabeth was finished. She looked at Jessica and smiled, and Jessica felt a warm glow of happiness. She knew the real Elizabeth was back.

"I know I still have to be punished for disobeying," Elizabeth said to her parents. "But I wanted to apologize for being so crazy about that silly game."

"Apology accepted, Elizabeth," Mrs. Wakefield said with a smile.

"I know what Liz's punishment should be," Jessica spoke up.

"What? Doing your chores?" said Steven, the twins' older brother. He smiled, his mouth full of creamed corn.

"Thank you, Steven," Mr. Wakefield said. "It's always a treat to eat dinner with you." Everyone laughed. "So what should Elizabeth's punishment be, Jessica?"

Jessica grinned at her sister. "Elizabeth has to help me make my story as good as hers, just like she promised."

"It's a deal," Elizabeth said. "Even

though I don't think you need much help."

Mrs. Wakefield nodded. "I think that sounds like a fair punishment."

Jessica breathed a sigh of relief. "Good. Can we eat now? I'm so hungry, I'm goin' wild!"

As soon as she got to school the next day, Jessica proudly turned in her composition for the Valentine's Day writing contest. She looked at her sister and smiled. "I bet one of us is going to win for sure," she said. "Thanks for helping me."

As the twins sat down at their desks, Andy and Todd came running over. "Hey, Elizabeth," Todd said. "Guess what? I'm almost to level five."

Jessica held her breath to see what Elizabeth would say.

"That's nice, Todd," Elizabeth said.

"Hey, where's your game?" Andy asked.

"I left it at home," Elizabeth told him.

"I bet I outscore you today," Todd boasted.

Elizabeth looked at Jessica and grinned. Then she looked up at the boys and shrugged. "That's nice."

Todd and Andy both looked so shocked that the twins burst into laughter.

"Jessica," Elizabeth said. "Let's go on the seesaw at recess today. I want to do something that takes two people to play!"

Todd came running over to the seesaw

67

at recess. "I just heard some teachers talking about the soap-box derby," he told Elizabeth, who was pushing up on the seesaw. Jessica was on the other end. "This is the first year we can enter. I'm going to build a *really* fast car."

"It's going to be a lot of fun," Elizabeth agreed. "Right, Jess?"

Jessica let her feet graze the ground so that the seesaw balanced perfectly. "I'm entering for sure."

"We can build identical cars," Elizabeth said. "And wear matching outfits."

"Maybe you'll even cross the finish line at the same time," Todd said. "Behind the winner—me."

Jessica laughed. "I don't know about

that, Todd. Twins are a team for life. A *winning* team."

Will Jessica and Elizabeth stay a team, or will something drive them apart? Find out in Sweet Valley Kids #37, THE BIG RACE.

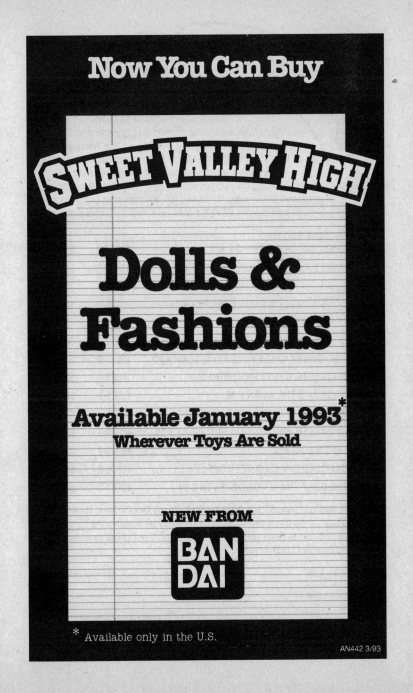

SWEET VALLEY KIDS

Jessica and Elizabeth have had lots of adventures in *Sweet Valley High* and *Sweet Valley Twins*...now read about the twins at age seven! You'll love all the fun that comes with being seven—birthday parties, playing dress-up, class projects, putting on puppet shows and plays, losing a tooth, setting up lemonade stands, caring for animals and much more! It's all part of SWEET VALLEY KIDS. Read them all!

☐	JESSICA AND THE SPELLING-BEE SURPRISE #21	15917-8	$2.75
☐	SWEET VALLEY SLUMBER PARTY #22	15934-8	$2.99
☐	LILA'S HAUNTED HOUSE PARTY # 23	15919-4	$2.99
☐	COUSIN KELLY'S FAMILY SECRET # 24	15920-8	$2.99
☐	LEFT-OUT ELIZABETH # 25	15921-6	$2.99
☐	JESSICA'S SNOBBY CLUB # 26	15922-4	$2.99
☐	THE SWEET VALLEY CLEANUP TEAM # 27	15923-2	$2.99
☐	ELIZABETH MEETS HER HERO #28	15924-0	$2.99
☐	ANDY AND THE ALIEN # 29	15925-9	$2.99
☐	JESSICA'S UNBURIED TREASURE # 30	15926-7	$2.99
☐	ELIZABETH AND JESSICA RUN AWAY # 31	48004-9	$2.99
☐	LEFT BACK! #32	48005-7	$2.99
☐	CAROLINE'S HALLOWEEN SPELL # 33	48006-5	$2.99
☐	THE BEST THANKSGIVING EVER # 34	48007-3	$2.99

Bantam Books, Dept. SVK2, 2451 S. Wolf Road, Des Plaines, IL 60018

Please send me the items I have checked above. I am enclosing $_____ (please add $2.50 to cover postage and handling). Send check or money order, no cash or C.O.D.s please.

Mr/Ms _____

Address _____

City/State _____ Zip _____

SVK2-11/92

Please allow four to six weeks for delivery.
Prices and availability subject to change without notice.